STICKMEN'S GUIDE TO YOUR MUSCLES AND BONES

by John Farndon
Illustrated by Venitia Dean

HUNGRY
TOMATO™

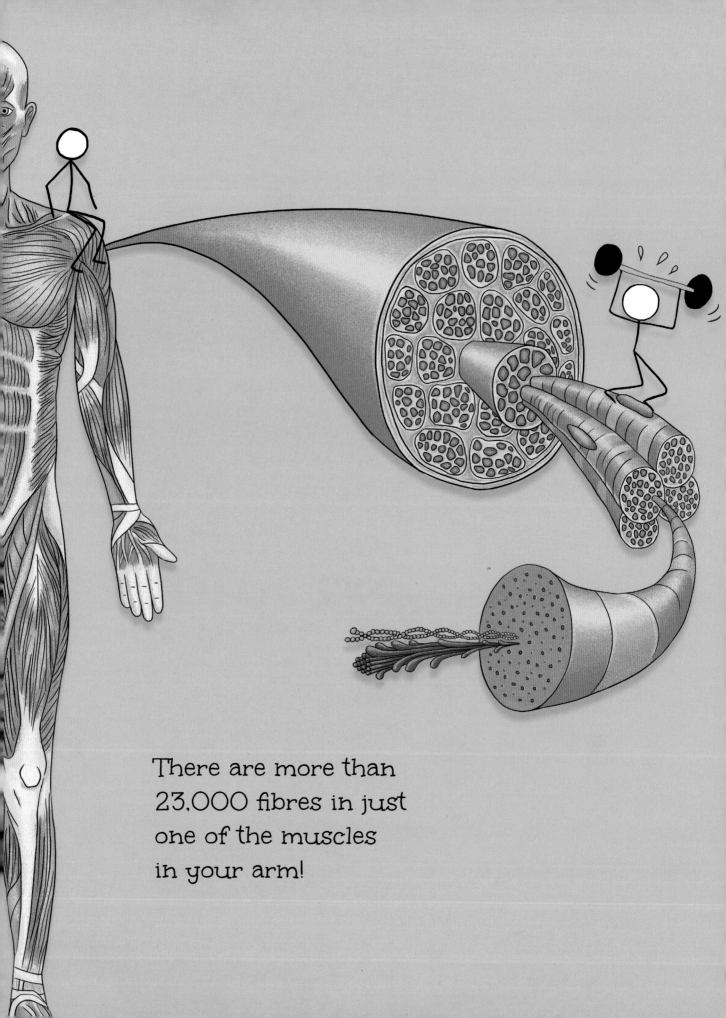

There are more than
23,000 fibres in just
one of the muscles
in your arm!

STICKMEN'S GUIDE TO YOUR MUSCLES AND BONES

Thanks to the creative team:

Senior editor: Alice Peebles
Fact checking: Kate Mitchell
Design: www.collaborate.agency

First published in Great Britain in 2017
by Hungry Tomato Ltd
PO Box 181
Edenbridge
Kent, TN8 9DP

Copyright © 2017 Hungry Tomato Ltd

A CIP catalogue record for this book is
available from the British Library.

ISBN 978-1-910684-87-0

Printed and bound in China

Contents

Introduction   6

Holding You Together   8

Your Muscly Body   10

Pulling Together   12

Inside a Muscle   14

How to Get Strong   16

Your Framework of Bones   18

Strong Bones   20

Moving Parts   22

Binders   24

Bonehead   26

The History of Muscle and Bone   28

More Muscly and Bony Facts   30

Index   32

Introduction

Although your body seems very complicated, it all begins to make sense if you think of it in terms of systems, each with its own task to do. Some extend throughout the body like the nervous system, which is the body's communication system. It is the task of the skeleton - the body's framework of bones - to protect you and keep you upright. The skeleton works in conjunction with muscles, which give your body the power to move.

Skeleton

The skeleton is the one part of the body that may survive after people die. That's because the hard bits of bones are made from tough minerals, which don't rot away like the rest. Altogether, over 100 billion people have lived on Earth so far. That means there could be 100 billion skeletons lying around. Fortunately, most do crumble into dust eventually!

Lucy

The world's most famous skeleton is about 3.2 million years old! It's called Lucy and is the skeleton of a small ancestor of humans called an australopithecine. It was found in Ethiopia in 1974. Its shape shows that even this long ago, our ancestors walked upright on two feet.

Muscles

You have over 600 muscles on the outside of your skeleton. If they could all pull together, they could lift a bus! Of course, that could never happen, because they all pull in different directions. The average adult man can just about lift another adult off the ground.

The strongest man

The world's strongest man ever was Canadian Louis Cyr, who lived between 1863 and 1912. He could push a railway truck uphill, beat two horses in a tug of war, and lift the weight of five adults with his little finger. His most famous feat was the backlift, in which he lifted a bench, with 18 men on it, on his back.

Meaty muscle

If you want to know what your muscles look like on the inside, go to the butcher. When you eat meat, you're eating mostly the muscle of animals. Only fat, gristle and bone are not muscle. If you ever eat steak, the chances are you'll be eating the big 'rump' or bottom muscles of a cow. Your own bottom muscles look much the same!

Holding You Together

If you looked through a powerful microscope, you would see that your body is made of tiny living packets called cells – about 37 trillion altogether! And just as lots of bricks make a wall, so lots of cells joined together make different kinds of tissue. Tissues are the basic building materials of your body.

Four tissues

There are four kinds of tissue. Most of you is either muscle tissue – the tissue that makes muscle – or 'connective' tissue, which fills the space between muscle and other tissues. But there are also small amounts of 'epithelial' tissue that line and wrap things, and nervous tissue that makes the nervous system, your body's internet.

Nervous tissue makes up your nerves and brain

Epithelial tissue lines your airways and blood vessels and wraps your heart

Connective tissue comes in various kinds, including bone, tendon, cartilage, fat and blood

Connective tissue

Connective tissue is made of three things: cells, thin fibres, and a 'matrix'. The matrix is basically just a setting for the other materials, like the bread in a currant loaf. It can be anything from a runny syrup to a thick gel.

Muscle tissue is the special fibres that make things move

Smooth muscle

There are different kinds of muscle. Smooth muscles are the ones deep inside your body. They form tubes or bags, and move things around by squeezing. Rings of smooth muscle squeeze food through your gut, for example.

Skeletal muscle

Skeletal muscles are all the muscles you see under your skin covering your skeleton. They are sometimes called 'striated' muscles. Striated means stripy and they get the name because under a microscope you can see dark bands around them.

Cardiac muscle

Cardiac muscle makes the strong walls of your heart. It squeezes automatically 100 or so times a minute to pump blood around your body. It is made from a mix of smooth and striated muscle.

Do it yourself

When you decide to jump and kick, your skeletal muscles make it happen. YOU can move these muscles if you want to, so they are called voluntary muscles. But you have little control over the heart and other muscles inside your body, so they are called involuntary muscles.

Your Muscly Body

Your body is covered with skeletal muscles. They are all bundles of fibres that tense and relax to move parts of your body. They range from big muscles, like those in your bottom and legs, to tiny muscles, such as those in your ear.

The skeletal muscles

You have 640 skeletal muscles altogether, and they make up two-fifths of your weight. In these diagrams, you only see the muscles on the surface, but there are several layers underneath. Some are long with a bulge in the middle, some are triangular, and some are sheet-like.

A major neck muscle, the sternocleidomastoid, tilts your head on either side

The pectoral turns your arm

The biceps raises your arm

The triceps lowers your arm

The external oblique holds your side in

The sartorius is the longest muscle in the body

The quadriceps bends your knee

The shin muscle lowers your foot

The sartorius moves both the hip and knee joint

Long muscle

The sartorius runs over the hip and down over the knee and turns the thigh. It gets its name from the Latin word *sartor*, meaning tailor. That's because tailors used to stretch this muscle when sitting cross-legged to work.

Strong jaw

It's not very big, but it's very strong – that's the masseter muscle that works your jaw. That's why you can really crunch down hard when you bite.

Masseter muscle

The trapezius muscle pulls your head back

The deltoid lifts your arm

The broadest back muscle, the latissimus dorsi, holds your back in place

The gluteus maximus holds your hip in place

The calf muscle lifts your ankle

Leg power

Your legs have your biggest muscles. They have to, because they hold you up, and they propel your body when you're running and jumping. At the top of your legs is the biggest pair of all, the gluteus maximus, your buttock muscles.

Pulling Together

Your muscles make your body move in all kinds of ways. But they do it all just by pulling themselves shorter (contracting) or relaxing. Each muscle works simply by pulling two bones together, so they must be anchored to bones at both ends.

Hamstrings draw your legs back

Calf muscles provide a spring push-off

Foot flexors lift the toes and feet

Core muscles provide a firm centre

Buttock muscles pull back and keep you stable

Hip muscles swing your hips forward

The quadriceps lift both legs up and forward

Moving together

Most movements, like running and jumping, involve an array of dozens of muscles, all pulling different parts of the body to make it move in the way you want. But you have to learn the programme to move all these muscles together. That's why toddlers aren't very good at it!

Muscle pairs

Muscles can make themselves shorter, but they cannot make themselves longer. So each time a muscle pulls shorter, it must usually be pulled back by another shortening in the opposite direction. That's why muscles are arranged in pairs - with a 'flexor' to bend a joint and an 'extensor' to straighten it out.

The triceps at the back of your arm shortens to pull your arm down again

The biceps at the front of your arm shortens to pull your arm up

Press-up

Press-ups are one of the simplest and most effective forms of exercise, which is why they are very popular with people wanting to keep fit. They involve most of the muscles in the upper body, including those in the arms, chest and abdomen.

Deltoids are the shoulder muscles that provide a firm base for the arms

Pectorals are the large upper chest muscles that really take the strain

Abdominal muscles help to hold the body steady

Inside a Muscle

Skeletal muscles get their strength from bundles of fibres that stretch from one end of the muscle to the other. Some muscles are made from just a few hundred fibres. Others are made from hundreds of thousands. But their superpower is getting shorter!

Bundle of muscle fibres

Muscle fibre

Myofibril

Muscle fibres

Muscles are built up from fibres, which are actually long cells. Each fibre is made from many, even thinner threads called myofibrils. These in turn are made from thin threads of two proteins: actin and myosin.

Actin

Myosin

Power packs

Myofibrils are built up from tiny power packs called sarcomeres. Inside them, thin, twisty strands of actin interlock with thicker, smoother strands of myosin. When you want to move, a nerve signal fires the muscle to act. At once, hooks on the myosin twist sharply and pull on the actin, shortening the muscle.

Muscle relaxed

Muscle contracted

Myosin

Actin

Pulling or holding

When a muscle moves part of the body, it shortens. This happens when you run, for example, and is called an 'isotonic contraction'. Sometimes, though, the muscles can pull to hold the body in place without getting shorter (below). This is an 'isometric contraction'.

Pulling
(Isotonic contraction)

Holding
(Isometric contraction)

Tendon

Muscle contracts and shortens

Muscle contracts but does not shorten

Holding weight

When muscles contract, they can shorten by almost half their length. When muscles work isometrically, however, they simply get fatter and stay the same length. This happens when a weightlifter holds the bar still overhead.

How to Get Strong

Top athletes and sportspeople train hard to get strong. They work hard at exercises that make their muscles grow, and better able to keep pulling. If muscles aren't used, they gradually become weaker.

Weight training

When you exercise you get fitter and stronger. Regular exercise improves fitness by bulking up your muscles, strengthening your heart and building up your body's ability to pump blood and supply muscles with oxygen. Weightlifters concentrate on building up their muscles for maximum strength. Marathon runners focus on endurance.

How a weightlifter's body shape changes as the muscles grow

Muscle growth

When you exercise, your muscles grow larger. At first, the fibres just get fatter. But if you go on exercising regularly, you grow new fibres, so your muscles become stronger. The blood supply to the muscles improves, so they can work for longer.

Untrained muscle

Trained muscle with new muscle fibres

Fast or slow?

Muscle fibres come in two kinds: white and red. Each kind pulls or 'twitches' at different rates. Sprinters have lots of white fibres that twitch rapidly to give a burst of action. Marathon runners develop slow-twitch red fibres that keep working longer.

Slow reds for marathons

Mix of whites and reds for middle distance

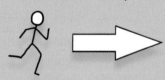
Fast whites for sprints

Air power

Muscle cells get their power from sugar in your food and the oxygen you breathe. On a long cycle ride, they work slowly and 'aerobically'. That means they work gently enough to take in air as they go. But when you sprint, your muscles work so fast your body can't deliver enough fresh oxygen. So they briefly work anaerobically (without air).

Cramps

If you're unfit, your muscles go on working anaerobically longer. Lactic acid builds up, making your muscles feel sore. You might also get cramp. A cramp is a painful twinge in your muscles. It is set off when the nerves that trigger them fire erratically. This is usually because of a temporary shortage of the minerals your nerves need to work properly.

Your Framework of Bones

Under your skin and muscles, you have a strong framework of bones called a skeleton. It holds your body together; provides anchor points for the muscles you use to move; supports your skin and other tissues; and protects your heart, brain and other organs.

Human skeleton

Your skeleton is made of over 200 bones. Your skull, spine and ribcage make the 'axial' skeleton. Your shoulders, arms, hands, hips, legs and feet are attached to this and form the 'appendicular' skeleton.

Finger bones or phalanges

Metacarpals

Hand bones

The hands each have 27 bones, making almost a quarter of all your bones. That's why hands can move in cleverer ways than any other part of your body. The hand bones form joints at the knuckles.

Wrist bones or carpals

Cheekbone

Collarbone

Breastbone or sternum

Thigh bone or femur

Kneecap or patella

Shin bone or tibia

Calf bone or fibula

Head office

Humans have rounded skulls like no other animals. Experts can track how humans developed in the distant past from the changing shape of ancient skulls they have found. They can see how the top, or cranium, grew to allow room for a bigger brain.

18

Skull

Shoulder blade or scapula

Ribs

Spine

Hip bone or pelvis

Spine tip or coccyx

Disc of cartilage

Feet bones

The feet each have 26 bones. These form three sets of bones: phalanges, metatarsals and tarsals.

Tarsals form three strong arches: two lengthways and one across your foot

Heel bone

Ankle bone or talus

Metatarsals

Toe bones or phalanges

Backbone

Your backbone, or spine, is the row of 33 linked bones down your back. The bones, or vertebrae, are drum-shaped and separated by a thin disc of jelly-like cartilage. There is just enough movement between them to let your back bend. With practice, gymnasts can bend their backs a long way.

Strong Bones

Bones are really light because they're partly hollow. But they're superstrong, too, because they're made of both hard minerals and stretchy fibres that stop them snapping.

Looking inside

Bones are complicated! The outside is a tough case of dense bone called 'compact' bone. This is reinforced by long rods called osteons. The inside is spongy and criss-crossed by bony supporting struts called trabeculae. Down the middle is a soft mass called marrow.

Yellow bone marrow

The periosteum or membrane wrapping the bone

Compact bone

Spongy bone

Arteries supply bones with nutrients

Lacuna containing osteoblast

Bone cells

Bones are full of pockets called lacunae. Each contains a living cell called an osteoblast, which is forever at work making new bone material. There are also bone cells called osteoclasts – the clean-up guys in the bone's interior, ready to clear away old bone material.

Marrow

Red blood cells

White blood cells

Platelets

Blood factory

The hollow centre of your bones contains a soft, spongy substance called marrow. Some is red and bloody, some yellow and fatty. Red marrow is the body's blood factory, churning out new blood cells non-stop.

Stickman

Bone

Steel

Bone v. steel

People sometimes say that bone is stronger than steel, weight for weight! That's not quite true: steel is stronger and bone is also very light, so a rod of steel the same size would be much stronger than bone. All the same, bone is both strong and very light – just what you need for moving around.

Broken bones

Bones are strong, but sometimes they do get broken. Amazingly, though, most fractures heal. First the body stops any bleeding. Then proteins summon osteoclasts to clear away the debris, so osteoblasts can begin to create new bone material to heal the fracture.

Moving Parts

Even though it is incredibly strong, your skeleton can bend and move in almost any direction thanks to its joints. Joints are where bones meet. All your bones, except one (the hyoid bone in your throat), form a joint with another bone.

Swivel joint

The swivel joint in your neck allows you to turn your head to the left and right.

Hinge joints

The hinge joints in your fingers, elbows, ankles and toes swing in only two directions, just like a door on hinges – but they are very strong. You use hinge joints when you make a fist or curl your toes.

Ellipsoidal joints

There is an ellipsoidal joint at the base of each index finger. It lets you bend and extend this finger, and rock it from side to side.

Ball and socket joints

Your hip and shoulder joints are your most flexible joints. They are ball-and-socket joints which let you swing your arms and legs in lots of different directions.

Saddle joints

The joints at the base of your thumbs are saddle joints. In these, two saddle-shaped bones fit snugly together, and can rock to and fro and from side to side. They are strong but can't rotate much.

Gliding joints

Where two flat bones are held together by ligaments just loosely enough to glide past each other, it's called a gliding joint. Some of the bones in your wrists and ankles move like this.

Muscle

Tendon

End of thigh bone or femur

Fluid

Cartilage

Top of shin bone or tibia

Joint capsule

Knee joint

Your knee is a special hinge joint. It can bend like all hinge joints, but can also rotate slightly. It's protected by a little shield of bone called the kneecap, and surrounded by a capsule of rubbery cartilage and fluid to cushion and lubricate it.

Knee injury

Knee joints are particularly vulnerable to damage. Many sportspeople suffer knee injuries that bring about major career setbacks. One of the most common is ligament injury caused by turning the knee sharply.

Bending bones?

Ligaments usually restrict the movement of your skeleton. But with practice, some 'contortionists' are able to stretch them and bend their bodies into all kinds of strange shapes. But the bones are not bending – it is just the joints moving further than normal.

23

Binders

Bones are tied together and muscles are tied to bones with short, strong fibres called ligaments and tendons. Ligaments are attached to the bones on either side of a joint and bind them together. Tendons anchor muscles to bones.

Hand holding

Your hand contains lots of strong ligaments and tendons to give you a strong grip. The muscles that move your fingers are not in your hand at all, but in your arm and connected by tendons. If you splay your fingers out, you can see these tendons clearly as ridges in the back of your hand. The diagram shows the palm of the hand.

Pretendinous bands pull your fingers up

Abductor muscles in the palm spread your hands

The palmaris longus tendon runs from a muscle in your arm to your hand

Shoulder blade

Triceps

Arm bands

The muscles in your arm are attached to bones via tendons at either end. The biceps is attached with a tendon to a part of the radius bone called the radial tuberosity, a small bump on the bone near your elbow joint.

Tendon

Biceps

Radial tuberosity

Radius bone

Shin muscle tendon

Toe tendon

Long calf muscle tendon

Big toe tendon

Plantar fascia ligament

Super strong

The tendons and ligaments in your feet have to be especially strong, since they must bear your entire weight, and provide the spring in your foot for running and jumping. The key ligament is the plantar fascia, which gives your foot its arch. By stretching and contracting, it allows the arch to curve or flatten, so you can balance and walk.

Achilles heel

When Ancient Greek hero Achilles was a baby, his mother dipped him in a magic river to make him invulnerable. But the water never reached the place on his heel where she held him. Later, he died in battle from a wound inflicted there. That's why the tendon holding your foot is called the Achilles tendon – but it is actually pretty strong!

Tear in Achilles tendon

Achilles tendon

Cartilaginous joints

Cartilage is the amazing rubbery material that cushions the ends of bones and stops them being damaged. And under your skin, your ears and nose are made of a special kind of extra bendy cartilage called elastic cartilage.

Bonehead

Your skull is the tough dome of bone that protects your brain. It looks like a single bone, but it is actually made from 22 bones cemented together by rigid joints called sutures.

Parietal bone on top of the skull

Suture

Fontanelle

Forehead or frontal bone

Cranium

Two parietal bones form the sides and top of the cranium

Occipital bone forms the back of the skull

Baby case

When you're born, the bones of your skull are not fixed together. That way they can slide over each other and overlap to let your head squeeze through your mum's birth canal. For a while after you're born, your skull has soft spots called fontanelles, which gradually fuse and harden.

Inside your head

Your skull provides such effective protection for your head that it's hard to know what's happening inside. That's why X-rays and brain scans are so important. They allow doctors and scientists to see inside, check for damage and learn more about what's going on.

Nut case

The dome at the top of your head that holds your brain is called the cranium. It's made of eight curved pieces of bone fused together along sutures. The rest of the skull comprises the 14 bones of your face. This includes your lower jaw, the only bone in your skull that moves.

The temporal bones on the sides of the skull house the ear structures

Suture

Forehead or frontal bone protects the brain and supports the face

Eye socket

Nose bone

Cheekbone

Upper jaw or maxilla

Lower jaw or mandible

Hole in the head

In ancient times, many people were 'trepanned'. Trepanning meant drilling a large hole in your skull. It was very dangerous, and must have been incredibly painful. No one knows just why they did it. Maybe they thought it would stop people suffering fits, or let evil spirits out.

Helmet

Your skull provides very strong protection for your vulnerable and delicate brain. Yet even your skull may not be enough if you hit your head hard. That's why safety helmets are vital when you ride a bike, or play sports where you can fall hard.

The History of Muscle and Bone

For a long time, scientists knew very little about muscle and bone. It seemed so obvious and simple, no one bothered to find out much. Only artists looked at muscles carefully, to understand how to draw people accurately. But gradually, scientists realized that there is quite a lot to learn about your skeleton and your muscles!

162 CE
The Roman physician Galen correctly identified the femur (thigh bone) as the longest and strongest bone in the body. But as bones are white, he thought they were made of white body fluids that had gone solid.

1630
The French thinker René Descartes began to look further into how muscles worked. He thought in terms of machines. He described muscles and tendons as 'devices and springs which serve to set [nerves] in motion'.

---

500 CE   **1600**   **1700**

1653
The English doctor William Harvey was the first to describe muscles as bundles of fibres. He also understood that they gave their power by contracting (shortening) and relaxing.

1510
The great Italian artist Leonardo da Vinci created amazingly accurate drawings of muscle and bone. He cut up bodies and studied them with his extraordinary eye for detail. Electronic body scans have shown just how accurate he was.

1543
The Italian physician Andreas Vesalius was one of the first to cut up dead bodies in order to map them scientifically. His famous book, *On the Fabric of the Human Body*, contained the first detailed and accurate drawings of all the bones of the skeleton and all the muscles.

1792

In Japan, people were not allowed to keep real skeletons. So doctors in training learned all about the bones of the skeleton from wooden models called *hoshino*.

1864

The German scientist Wilhelm Kühne discovered the protein myosin, one of the two key proteins that make muscles contract. He thought it occurred only when the muscle is contracted.

1954

The British scientist Andrew Huxley and others worked out that muscles contract as filaments (threads) of myosin and actin slide over each other. This is called the 'sliding filament' theory.

1942

The Hungarian scientist Brunó Straub discovered actin, the other key protein that makes muscles contract.

1800

1900

2000

1895

The German physicist Wilhelm Röntgen discovered how X-ray photographs could see right inside a body and take pictures of bones in living people for the first time. X-rays make it easy for doctors to see if a bone is broken.

1968

Bone marrow is where new blood cells are made. So any damage to bone marrow can have a damaging effect on health. In 1968, the transplant of healthy marrow into a damaged bone was successfully done for the first time.

1940s

The Hungarian-American scientist Albert Szent-Györgyi began to explore how different chemicals played a part in explaining how muscles contract.

More Muscly and Bony Facts

Neck and neck

The sternocleidomastoid is a large muscle running down the side of your neck. It's pronounced stern-o-cly-doe-mass-toid. This is the muscle that swivels your head, and it's unique to humans. So when film-makers want to create a 'good' alien, they often include this muscle to help you identify with the character.

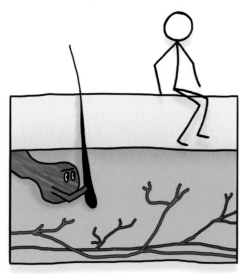

Muscle count

No one actually knows how many muscles there are in the human body. It all depends on how you count them. Massage specialists deal with about 200–300 skeletal muscles. Specialist anatomists might be able to identify another 400 or so. Then there are millions of muscles that raise hairs, and billions of smooth muscles deep inside the body, such as those in the gut.

Bone count

No one knows exactly how many bones you have right now! That's your body's secret. When you're born you have about 300, but as you grow, some of these bones fuse together. So by the time you're an adult you'll have just 206. Your bones also become denser and heavier until you're about 30 years old.

The quiet muscle

The tensor tympani is a tiny muscle in each of your ears. Its job is to pull on the tiny 'hammer' bone in your ear and stop the bone rattling when you're chewing. That way you aren't deafened by the sound of your own mouth... It also stops your ears getting damaged when you yell too loudly!

Sleep power

We know how exercise can make your muscles grow. But *when* do the muscles actually grow after that tough workout? It seems that this happens when you fall into a deep sleep, so your muscles relax, allowing more blood to flow and the hormones that stimulate muscle growth to circulate.

Hot muscle

Your muscles create a lot of your body heat. When muscles contract, they generate a lot of warmth. That's why you shiver when you are cold. Your body is trying to warm you up by rapidly contracting and relaxing muscles.

Funny bone

People often talk of hitting their 'funny bone'. Actually it's not a bone at all. It's the ulnar nerve, which runs across your elbow on the inside. Accidentally bumping it sets off a strange, tingling sensation and may even stop your hand working for a moment.

INDEX

A
Achilles heel 25
arms 12, 24

B
backbone 19
bodybuilders 16
bone cells 20
bone marrow 20, 21
bones 6, 18, 19, 30
    inside 20, 21
    joints 22, 23
    strength 20, 21

C
cardiac muscle 9
cartilage 25
connective tissue 8
cramps 17

E
ear muscles 31

F
feet 19, 25
funny bone 31

H
hands 18, 24
history of muscle and
    bone 28, 29

J
jaw 11, 27
joints 22, 23

K
knees 23

L
legs 10, 11
ligaments 24, 25
Lucy 6

M
muscle fibres 14, 18
muscle pairs 12
muscles 7, 30, 31
    growth 16, 17, 31
    inside 7, 14, 15
    moving 12, 13, 14, 15
    skeletal 9, 10, 11, 12, 13
    strength 16, 17
    types 8, 9

N
neck muscles 30

P
press-ups 13

R
runners 16, 17

S
shivering 31
skeletal muscles 9, 10, 11, 12, 13
skeleton 6, 18, 19, 30
    joints 22, 23
skull 18, 26, 27
strongest man 7

T
tendons 24, 25
tissue 8
trepanning 27

W
weightlifters 7, 15, 16

The Author

John Farndon is Royal Literary Fellow at City&Guilds in London, UK, and the author of a huge number of books for adults and children on science, technology and nature, including such international best-sellers as *Do Not Open* and *Do You Think You're Clever?* He has been shortlisted six times for the Royal Society's Young People's Book Prize for a science book, with titles such as *How the Earth Works, What Happens When?* and *Project Body* (2016).

The Illustrator

Venitia Dean is a freelance illustrator who grew up in Brighton, UK. She has always loved drawing ever since she could hold a pencil! As a teenager she discovered a passion for figurative illustration and when she turned 19 she was given a digital drawing tablet for her birthday and started transferring her work to the computer. She hasn't looked back since! As well as illustration, Venitia loves reading graphic novels, and walking her dog Peanut.